Paddington
in the
Garden

First published in hardback by HarperCollins Publishers, USA, in 2002
First published in hardback in Great Britain by Collins in 2002
Revised edition published in paperback by HarperCollins Children's Books in 2008
This edition published in 2014

12

ISBN: 978-0-00-712316-2

Collins is an imprint of HarperCollins Publishers Ltd.
HarperCollins Children's Books is a division of HarperCollins Publishers Ltd.

A CIP catalogue record for this title is available from the British Library.

Visit our website at: www.harpercollins.co.uk

Printed in China

Michael Bond

Paddington in the Garden

Illustrated by R. W. Alley

HarperCollins *Children's Books*

One morning Paddington went out into the garden and began making a list of all the nice things he could think of about being a bear and living with the Browns.

He had a room of his own and a warm bed to sleep in. And he had marmalade for breakfast *every* morning. In Darkest Peru he had only been allowed it on Sundays.

The list was soon so long he had nearly run out of paper before he realised he had left out one of the nicest things of all...

…the garden itself!

Apart from the occasional noise from a nearby building site, it was so quiet and peaceful it didn't seem like being in London at all.

But nice gardens don't just happen. They usually require a lot of hard work, and the one at number thirty-two Windsor Gardens was no exception. Mr Brown had to mow the lawn twice a week, and Mrs Brown was kept busy weeding the flower beds. There was always something to do. Even Mrs Bird lent a hand whenever she had a spare moment.

It was Mrs Bird who first suggested giving Jonathan, Judy and Paddington each a piece of the garden.

"It will keep certain bears out of mischief," she said meaningly. "And it will be fun for Jonathan and Judy as well."

Mr Brown agreed it was a very good idea, and he marked out three plots at the far end of the lawn.

Paddington was most excited. "I don't suppose there are many bears who have their own garden!" he exclaimed.

Early the next morning all three set to work.

Judy decided to make a flower bed and Jonathan had his eye on some old paving stones.

Paddington didn't know what to do. In the past he had often found that gardening was much harder than it looked, especially when you only had paws.

In the end, armed with a jar of Mrs Bird's home-made marmalade, he borrowed Mr Brown's wheelbarrow and set off to look for ideas.

His first stop was a stall in the market, where he bought a book called *How to Plan Your Garden* by Lionel Trug.

It came complete with a large packet of assorted seeds, and if the picture on the front cover was anything to go by, it was no wonder Mr Trug looked happy for he seemed to do most of his planning while lying in a hammock. By the end of the book, without lifting a finger, he was surrounded by blooms.

Paddington decided it was very good value indeed – especially when the owner of the stall gave him two pence change.

ANTIQUES
R·6

Mr Trug's book was full of useful hints and tips.

The first one suggested that before starting work it was a good idea to close your eyes and try to picture what the garden would look like when it was finished.

Having walked into a lamppost by mistake, Paddington decided to read another page or two, and there he found a much better idea. Mr Trug advised standing back and looking at the site from a safe distance, preferably somewhere high up.

He knew just the spot.

By the time Paddington reached the building site near the Browns' house it was the middle of the morning, and the men were all at their tea break.

Placing his jar of marmalade on a wooden platform for safekeeping, he sat on a pile of bricks for a rest while he considered the matter.

There was no one about...

And there was a ladder nearby...

Mr Trug was quite right. The Browns' garden did look very different from high up. But before he had time to get his breath back, Paddington heard the sound of an engine starting up. He peered through a gap in the boards. As he did so his eyes nearly popped out.

On the ground just below him, a man was emptying a load of concrete on the very spot where he had left his jar of marmalade!

Paddington scrambled back down the ladder as fast as his legs would carry him, reaching the bottom just as the foreman came around a corner.

"Is anything wrong?" asked the man. "You look upset."

"My jar's been buried!" exclaimed Paddington hotly, pointing to the pile of concrete. "It had some of Mrs Bird's best golden chunks in it, too!"

"I won't ask how your jar got there," said the foreman, turning to Paddington as his men set to work clearing the concrete into small piles, "*or* what you were doing up the ladder."

"I'm glad of that," said Paddington, politely raising his hat.

Suddenly there was a whirring sound from somewhere overhead, and to Paddington's surprise the platform landed at his feet. "My marmalade!" he exclaimed thankfully.

"Your *marmalade*?" repeated the foreman, staring at the jar. "Did you say marmalade?"

"That's right," said Paddington. "I put it there ready for my elevenses. It must have been taken up by mistake. Now the top's come off!"

It was the foreman's turn to look as though he could hardly believe his eyes.

"That's special quick-drying cement!" he wailed.

"It's probably rock-hard already – ruined by a bear's marmalade! No one will give me tuppence for it now!"

"I will," said Paddington eagerly. "I've had an idea!"

Paddington was busy for the rest of the week.

When the builders saw the rock garden he had made, they were most impressed, and the foreman even gave him some plants to finish it off until his seeds started to grow.

"It's National Garden Day on Saturday," he said. "There are some very famous people judging it. I'll spread the word around. You never know your luck."

GARDEN
DAY
Saturday, May

The foreman was as good as his word, and on Saturday half the neighbourhood turned up at number thirty-two Windsor Gardens to see the judges arrive.

Paddington nearly fell over backwards with surprise when he discovered that no less a person than Mr Lionel Trug himself was leading the procession.

“It’s very good of you to get out of your hammock, Mr Trug!” he exclaimed.

“Er…not at all,” said Lionel Trug. “My pleasure. I must say, I love your orange stones. Where *did* you find them?”

“I didn’t,” said Paddington. “I think they found me. Thanks to the builders.”

"Congratulations!" said Mr Trug, as he handed Paddington a gold star. "It's good to see a young bear taking up gardening. I hope you will be the first of many."

"Who would have believed it?" said Mr Brown, as the last of the crowd departed.

"You must write and tell Aunt Lucy all about it," said Mrs Bird. "They'll be very excited in the Home for Retired Bears when they hear the news."

Paddington thought that was a good idea, but he had something to do first.

He wanted to add one more important item to his list of all the nice things there were about being a bear and living with the Browns:

HAVING MY OWN ROCK GARDEN!

Then he signed his name and added his special paw print...
...just to show it was genuine.